Geronimo Stilton
ENGLISH!

 **25 AT THE HARBOUR** 海港游

新雅文化事業有限公司
www.sunya.com.hk

Geronimo Stilton English
AT THE HARBOUR　海港遊

作　　者：Geronimo Stilton 謝利連摩・史提頓
譯　　者：申倩
責任編輯：王燕參
封面繪圖：Giuseppe Facciotto
插圖繪畫：Claudio Cernuschi, Andrea Denegri, Daria Cerchi
內文設計：Angela Ficarelli, Raffaella Picozzi
出　　版：新雅文化事業有限公司
　　　　　香港英皇道499號北角工業大廈18樓
　　　　　電話：（852）2138 7998
　　　　　傳真：（852）2597 4003
　　　　　網址：http://www.sunya.com.hk
　　　　　電郵：marketing@sunya.com.hk
發　　行：香港聯合書刊物流有限公司
　　　　　香港新界大埔汀麗路36號中華商務印刷大廈3字樓
　　　　　電話：（852）2150 2100　傳真：（852）2407 3062
　　　　　電郵：info@suplogistics.com.hk
印　　刷：C & C Offset Printing Co.,Ltd
　　　　　香港新界大埔汀麗路36號
版　　次：二〇一二年七月初版
　　　　　10 9 8 7 6 5 4 3 2 1

ISBN: 978-962-08-5622-8
© 2008 Edizioni Piemme S.p.A., Via Tiziano 32 - 20145 Milano - Italia
International Rights © 2007 Atlantyca S.p.A. - via Leopardi, 8, Milano - Italy
© 2012 for this Work in Traditional Chinese language, Sun Ya Publications (HK) Ltd.
18/F, North Point Industrial Building, 499 King's Road, Hong Kong.
Published and printed in Hong Kong

CONTENTS
目 錄

BENJAMIN'S CLASSMATES
班哲文的老師和同學們

Maestra Topitilla
托比蒂拉‧德‧托比莉斯

Rarin
拉琳

Diego
迪哥

Rupa
露芭

Tui
杜爾

David
大衞

Sakura
櫻花

Mohamed
穆哈麥德

Tian Kai
田凱

Oliver
奧利佛

Milenko
米蘭哥

Trippo
特里普

Carmen
卡敏

Atina
阿提娜

Esmeralda
愛絲梅拉達

Pandora
潘朵拉

Takeshi
北野

Kuti
菊花

Benjamin
班哲文

Hsing
阿星

Laura
羅拉

Kiku
奇哥

Antonia
安東妮婭

Liza
麗莎

GERONIMO AND HIS FRIENDS

謝利連摩和他的家鼠朋友們

謝利連摩·史提頓 Geronimo Stilton
一個古怪的傢伙，簡直可以說是一隻笨拙的文化鼠。他是
《鼠民公報》的總裁，正花盡心思改變報紙業的歷史。

菲·史提頓 Tea Stilton
謝利連摩的妹妹，她是《鼠民公報》的特派記者，同
時也是一個運動愛好者。

班哲文·史提頓 Benjamin Stilton
謝利連摩的小侄兒，常被叔叔稱作「我的
小乳酪」，是一隻感情豐富的小老鼠。

潘朵拉·華之鼠 Pandora Woz
柏蒂·活力鼠的姨甥女、班哲文最好的朋友，
是一隻活潑開朗的小老鼠。

柏蒂·活力鼠 Patty Spring
美麗迷人的電視新聞工作者，致力於她熱愛的電視事業。

賴皮 Trappola
謝利連摩的表弟，非常喜歡食物，風趣幽默，是一隻饞
嘴、愛開玩笑的老鼠，善於將歡樂傳遞給每一隻鼠。

麗萍姑媽 Zia Lippa
謝利連摩的姑媽，對鼠十分友善，又和藹可親，只想將
最好的給身邊的鼠。

艾拿 Iena
謝利連摩的好朋友，充滿活力，熱愛各項運動，他希望
能把對運動的熱誠傳給謝利連摩。

史奎克·愛管閒事鼠 Ficcanaso Squitt
謝利連摩的好朋友，是一個非常有頭腦的私家
偵探，總是穿着一件黃色的乾濕樓。

A SPECIAL DAY 特別的一天

親愛的小朋友，你喜歡乘帆船還是輪船呢？我以一千塊莫澤雷勒乳酪發誓，這對我來說沒什麼分別……因為我無論乘什麼船都會暈船！昨天我在港口碰見史柏力叔叔，他答應今天帶我和班哲文去遊覽妙鼠城海港，柏蒂和潘朵拉也會來。你也想一起來嗎？一定很好玩的！

Did you go to the harbour yesterday?
昨天你去港口了嗎？
Yes, I did.
是的，我去了。
No, I didn't.
不，我沒有去。

No, I didn't.

跟我謝利連摩‧史提頓一起學英文，
就像玩遊戲一樣簡單好玩！

你可以一邊看着圖畫一邊讀。
以下有幾個標誌，你要特別留意：

當看到 🔘 標誌時，你可以聽CD，
一邊聽，一邊跟着朗讀，還可以跟
着一起唱歌。

當看到 ★ 標誌時，你可以和朋友
們一起玩遊戲，或者嘗試回答問
題。題目很簡單，它們對鞏固你所
學過的內容很有幫助。

當看到 ❗ 標誌時，你要注意看一
下格子裏的生字，反覆唸幾遍，掌
握發音。

最後，不要忘記完成小測驗和練習
冊裏的問題！看看你有多聰明吧。

祝大家學得開開心心！

謝利連摩‧史提頓

LOOK AT ALL THOSE BOATS!
看看那些船！

一到港口，班哲文和潘朵拉就急不及待地想要四處遊覽，連柏蒂也急着想聽史柏力叔叔的介紹。只有我看起來有點擔心，難道是因為我看到港口停泊了那麼多船，已開始覺得暈船了嗎？

sailing boat

cruise ship

ship

crane

fishing boat

harbour

captain

sailor

cket office

harbour office

The fishing boat didn't go out to sea last night because there was a storm.

The sea is calm today. The fishing boat can go out to fish tonight.

how many　多少
there are　那兒有

9

OVER ONE HUNDRED
超過100

潘朵拉看見港口停泊了一艘郵輪，她很想知道這艘郵輪能載多少名乘客。「655名！」史柏力叔叔十分肯定地告訴她！這可是一個學習100以上的數字的好機會啊！小朋友，你也一起來學習吧！

100 one hundred

101 one hundred and one

102 one hundred and two

103 one hundred and three

104 one hundred and four

105 one hundred and five

106 one hundred and six

107 one hundred and seven

108 one hundred and eight

109 one hundred and nine

110 one hundred and ten

120 one hundred and twenty

130 one hundred and thirty

140 one hundred and forty

150 one hundred and fifty

160 one hundred and sixty

170 one hundred and seventy

180 one hundred and eighty

190 one hundred and ninety

200 two hundred

300 three hundred

400 four hundred

500 five hundred

600 six hundred

700 seven hundred

800 eight hundred

900 nine hundred

1,000 one thousand

10,000 ten thousand

100,000 one hundred thousand

1,000,000 one million

Uncle Spelliccio, how many passengers are there on the cruise ship?

How many people work in the harbour, Uncle Geronimo?

600, more or less! 655 to be precise!

Lots of people, about a thousand!

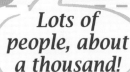

> **!** more or less
> 大約
> about a thousand
> 約1,000

 **A SONG FOR YOU!** Track 1

In the Harbour

How many boats are there in the harbour?
There must be 100 or 200,
they are yellow, red and blue
all together they go TOOT!!!

How many ferries are there in the harbour?
There must be 300 or 400,
they are yellow, red and blue
all together they go TOOT!!!

100, 200, 300 and more
400, 500 or 604!
All together they are into the sea,
all together they go TOOT TOOT!!!

How many fishing boats are there in the harbour?
There must be 500 or 600,
they are yellow, red and blue
all together they go TOOT!!!

TOPAZIA AQUARIUM
妙鼠城水族館

港口的旁邊有一個水族館——妙鼠城水族館，裏面飼養了很多七彩繽紛的魚兒和海洋生物，還有海豚表演呢。班哲文和潘朵拉很想去參觀，你也一起來吧。

In the aquarium there are many tanks with different kinds of fish.

The coral reef tank is one of the biggest and contains hundreds of colourful fish.

Penguins are excellent swimmers. They look as if they're flying underwater!

This pool contains many sea turtles. Sometimes, fishermen find them in their nets and bring them here. We take care of them then we take them back to sea.

我以一千塊莫澤雷勒乳酪發誓，海豚真的好聰明啊！
牠們能跳出水面，而且跳得很高。牠們還會噴水和玩球，
實在太厲害了！

They jump out of the water and dive back in!

The dolphins, at last!

They stay with us for a while, then we take them back to sea.

hundreds of　數以百計
at last　最後
for a while　一會兒

They are fantastic, aren't they?

Yes, they are friendly and playful!

WHAT TIME IS THE NEXT FERRY LEAVING?
下一班船什麼時候開出？

離開水族館後，班哲文和潘朵拉還想去參觀沉船，於是我買了4張船票，讓大家乘船出海去參觀沉在海底的海盜船。

A RIDE ON THE FERRY
渡輪之旅

我們很快就上了船。我和柏蒂告訴孩子們在船上要處處小心，並且要有禮貌。

★ 試着用英語説出：「不要大叫！」

答案：Don't shout!

班哲文和潘朵拉對船上的每樣東西都感到十分好奇。他們很想知道船上各個部分的英文名稱怎麼說，於是柏蒂拿出一張船的海報給他們看，並教他們用英語說出船上各個部分的名稱，你也跟着一起學習吧。

antenna

funnel

lifeboat

games area

cabin

porthole

restaurant

deck

I'm seasick.
我暈船。

propeller

Look, Uncle G, there's a restaurant, too!

Would you like to eat something Geronimo?

Well... I can't eat anything... I'm seasick!

WHAT IS OUR COURSE, CAPTAIN?
船長，我們的航行路線是什麼？

我在船上感到很不自在……惟一能讓我不去想暈船的事就是參觀船長室了。船長是一隻很健談的老鼠，他跟我說了很多關於航海的事。原來要做一名稱職的船員要知道的知識還真不少呢！

north

northeast

northwest

west

east

southwest

southeast

south

course 路線
rudder 船舵
compass 羅盤
breeze 微風
strong wind 大風
storm 暴風雨
gale 強風
hurricane 颶風

接着，船長帶我們來到一個特別的船艙裏，我們終於看到那艘沉船了，班哲文和潘朵拉感到十分興奮。他們聽着船長講述關於沉船殘骸和寶藏的故事，這個故事他們至少聽過一百萬遍了，可是，我以一千塊莫澤雷勒乳酪發誓，他們總是聽不厭的！

A SONG FOR YOU! Track 2

Would You Like to Be a Captain?

Would you like to be a captain and have your own ship?
Would you like to sail the seas

looking for hidden treasures?
With your imagination
you can sail the seven seas
have wonderful adventures
with your pirate crew.

| sunk | 沉沒 |
| found | 發現 |

19

〈紫羅蘭和薰衣草〉

麗萍姑媽的家。春天快到了。

麗萍姑媽：啊，我美麗的薰衣草呀！
謝利連摩：咳，咳！
史柏力：噓……安靜點！一定不能讓她發現我們的。

柏蒂：史柏力叔叔，你真是浪漫啊！
史柏力：謝謝，但是……噓，不要作聲！

史柏力：早晨，我們是來取從史柏力島運送過來的貨物的。
柏蒂：真是太浪漫了！
潘朵拉：接着我們應該做什麼呢？

史柏力：除了薰衣草外，麗萍最喜歡的花就是……紫羅蘭了！
眾老鼠：哦——！

謝利連摩：它們是由一個溫暖的地方運來的，那裏的紫羅蘭比其他地方早幾星期開花！
柏蒂：這是他用來作為他們結婚周年紀念的禮物。

Unfortunately, all the dockers are busy.

This is… pant… less romantic!

See the leaves? They are heart shaped!

Nice, but… can we have a break?

史柏力：看到那些葉子嗎？它們是心形的！
謝利連摩：很好看，但……我們可以休息一會兒嗎？

史柏力：真不巧，所有的搬運工人都沒空。
柏蒂：這就……呼……沒那麼浪漫了！

Five minutes later…

Shall we go then?

Ok, let's go!

五分鐘後……
班哲文：我們可以走了嗎？
謝利連摩：好，我們走吧！

But first have some violet tea: it'll make you really strong!

史柏力：但走之前先來喝一杯紫羅蘭花茶吧，它能令你變得非常強壯！

What does "say it with flowers" mean?

It means that each flower has a special meaning!

潘朵拉：「花語」是什麼意思？
柏蒂：它的意思是每一種花都有一個特別的意思。

班哲文：那紫羅蘭的意思是什麼？

謝利連摩：它的意思是……背痛嗎？

柏蒂：不，它代表回憶！

柏蒂：謝利連摩，你咳得很厲害呀！

謝利連摩：你知道怎樣才能令我好一點嗎？

史柏力：當然知道！

史柏力：紫羅蘭花茶！

謝利連摩：呀……嗯……謝謝！

柏蒂：我們到了！

史柏力：驚喜吧！

The End

麗萍姑媽：噢，謝謝你！為了慶祝這美好的時刻，我為你們準備了……一些紫羅蘭花茶！

柏蒂：太浪漫了！

謝利連摩：唉！

TEST 小測驗

⭐ 1. 下面的船隻用英語該怎麼說？說說看。

(a) 漁船　　**(b)** 渡輪　　**(c)** 快艇　　**(d)** 郵輪　　**(e)** 帆船

⭐ 2. 讀出下面的句子，然後用中文說出它們的意思。

(a) There are more than 100 boats!

(b) This is Topazia Harbour!

(c) The tank contains hundreds of fish.

(d) Penguins are excellent swimmers.

⭐ 3. 用英語說出下面的數字。

(a) 202　　**(b)** 220　　**(c)** 240　　**(d)** 250　　**(e)** 103

(f) 101　　**(g)** 405　　**(h)** 607　　**(i)** 1,000,000

⭐ 4. 讀出下面有關船上各部分的英文名稱，然後用中文說出它們的意思。

(a) propeller　　**(b)** porthole　　**(c)** deck

(d) lifeboat　　**(e)** cabin

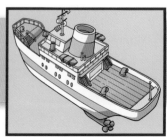

DICTIONARY 詞典

（英、粵、普發聲）

A

adventures　冒險

anniversary　周年紀念

antenna　天線

aquarium　水族館

at last　最後

B

backache　背痛

beautiful　美麗

because　因為

breakwater　防波堤

breeze　微風

C

cabin　船艙

calm　平靜

captain　船長

careful　小心

celebrate　慶祝

compass　羅盤

coral reef　珊瑚礁

cough　咳嗽

course　路線

crane　起重機

cruise ship　郵輪

D

deck　甲板

different　不同的

dive　潛水

divers　潛水員

dolphins　海豚

E

east 東

excellent 出色的

F

ferry 渡輪

fish 魚

fishermen 漁夫

fishing boat 漁船

for a while 一會兒

friendly 友善

funnel (輪船的) 煙囪

G

gale 強風

games area 遊戲區

gift 禮物

H

harbour 海港

harbour office 海港辦事處

hundreds of 數以百計

hurricane 颶風

I

imagination 想像力

J

jump 跳

K

kinds 種類

L

last night 昨晚

lavender 薰衣草

lifeboat 救生艇

lighthouse 燈塔

M

met 遇見

motorboat 快艇

museum 博物館

N

nets　網

north　北

northeast　東北

northwest　西北

O

oil tanker　運油輪

one hundred　一百

one million　一百萬

one thousand　一千

P

passengers　乘客

penguins　企鵝

pier　碼頭

pirate ship　海盜船

playful　愛玩耍

pool　水池

porthole　舷窗

precise　準確

propeller　螺旋槳

R

restaurant　餐廳

romantic　浪漫

rowing boat　划艇

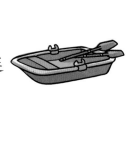

rudder　船舵

run　跑

S

sailing boat　帆船

sailor　水手

seasick　暈船

sea turtles　海龜

ship　輪船

shipwreck 沉船

shout 大聲叫

sometimes 有時

south 南

southeast 東南

southwest 西南

special 特別的

stay 停留

storm 暴風雨

strong wind 大風

sunk 沉沒

surprise 驚喜

swimmers 游泳員

today 今天

tonight 今晚

treasure 寶藏

tugboat 拖船

U

underwater 在水中

V

violets 紫羅蘭

W

wedding 結婚

west 西

T

tank 魚缸

ticket office 售票處

Y

yesterday 昨天

GERONIMO'S ISLAND
老鼠島地圖

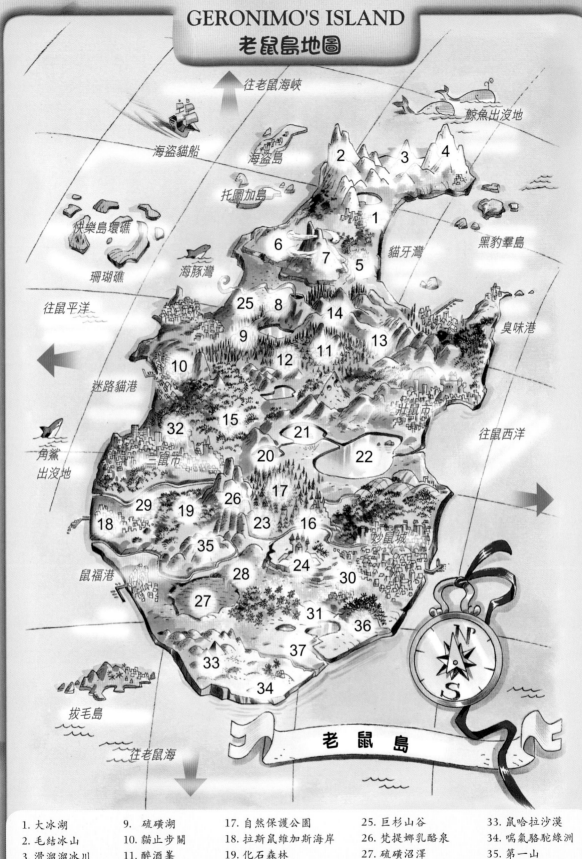

往老鼠海峽

鯨魚出沒地

海盜貓船　海盜島

托圖加島

快樂島環礁

珊瑚礁　海豚灣

往鼠平洋

迷路貓港

角鯊
出沒地

貓牙灣

黑豹羣島

臭味港

往鼠西洋

壯鼠市

三鼠市

妙鼠城

鼠福港

拔毛島

往老鼠海

老　鼠　島

Geronimo Stilton

EXERCISE BOOK
練習冊

想知道自己對 AT THE HARBOUR 掌握了多少，
趕快打開後面的練習完成它吧！

ENGLISH!

25 AT THE HARBOUR 海港遊

LOOK AT ALL THOSE BOATS! 看看那些船！

⭐ 港灣內停泊了很多不同的船隻，你知道它們的英文名稱嗎？從下面選出適當的字詞，填在橫線上。

motorboat	fishing boat	tugboat
cruise ship	sailing boat	ferry

1. _____

2. _____

3. _____

4. _____

5. _____

6. _____

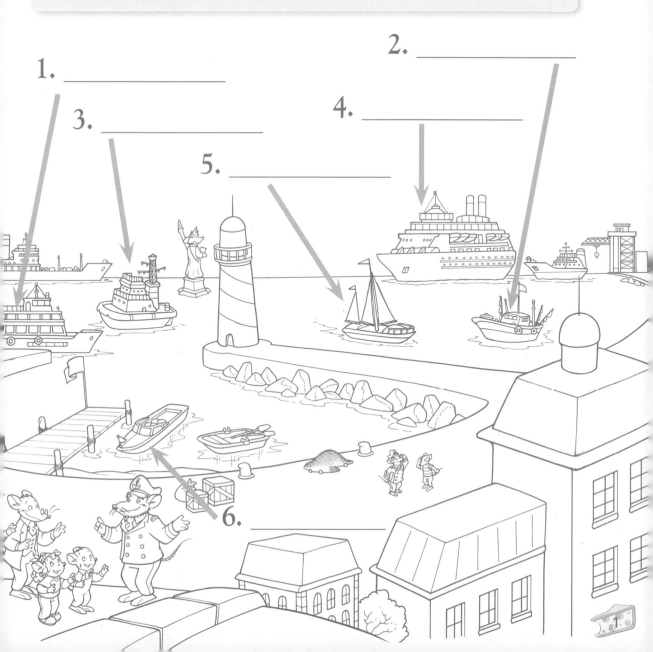

TOPAZIA HARBOUR
妙鼠城海港

⭐ 選出適當的字詞填在橫線上，完成句子。

1. The fishing _____ didn't go out to _____ last night _____ there was a _____ .

storm
boat
because
sea

fish
fishing
calm
go

2. The sea is _____ today. The _____ boat can _____ out to _____ tonight.

NUMBERS 數字

★ 看看下面的阿拉伯數字，這些數字用英語該怎麼說呢？在橫線上把它們的英文說法補寫完整。

1.　100 one _____	2.　110 one hundred and _____	3.　120 one hundred and _____
4.　130 one hundred and _____	5.　140 one hundred and _____	6.　150 one hundred and _____
7.　160 one hundred and _____	8.　170 one hundred and _____	9.　180 one hundred and _____
10.　190 one hundred and _____	11.　200 _____ hundred	12.　300 _____ hundred
13.　400 _____ hundred	14.　500 _____ hundred	15.　1,000 one _____
16.　10,000 _____ thousand	17.　100,000 one _____ thousand	18.　1,000,000 one _____

TOPAZIA AQUARIUM
妙鼠城水族館

⭐ 你還記得班哲文和潘朵拉在妙鼠城水族館裏看到些什麼嗎？從下面選出適當的字詞填在橫線上，完成句子。

aquarium	hundreds	fish
Penguins	turtles	

1.

In the _____ there are many tanks with different kinds of _____ .

2.

This tank contains _____ of colourful fish.

3.

_____ are excellent swimmers.

4.

This pool contains many sea _____ .

4

THE SHIP 輪船

★ 你知道輪船各部分的名稱用英語該怎麼說嗎？從下面選出適當的字詞，填在橫線上。

deck   porthole
funnel   propeller
lifeboat

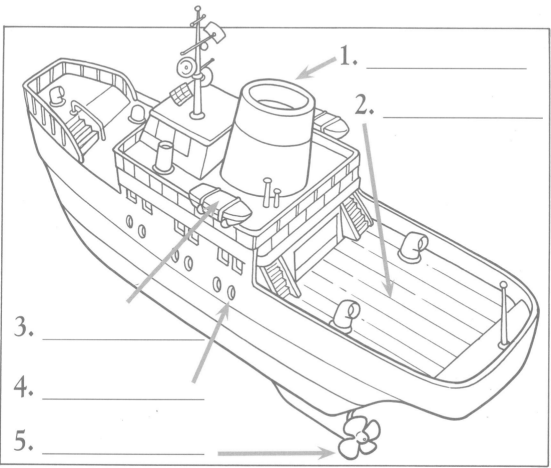

1. _____

2. _____

3. _____

4. _____

5. _____

CROSSWORD PUZZLE
字謎遊戲

⭐ 你知道下面這些字詞用英語該怎麼説嗎？完成下面的字謎遊戲。

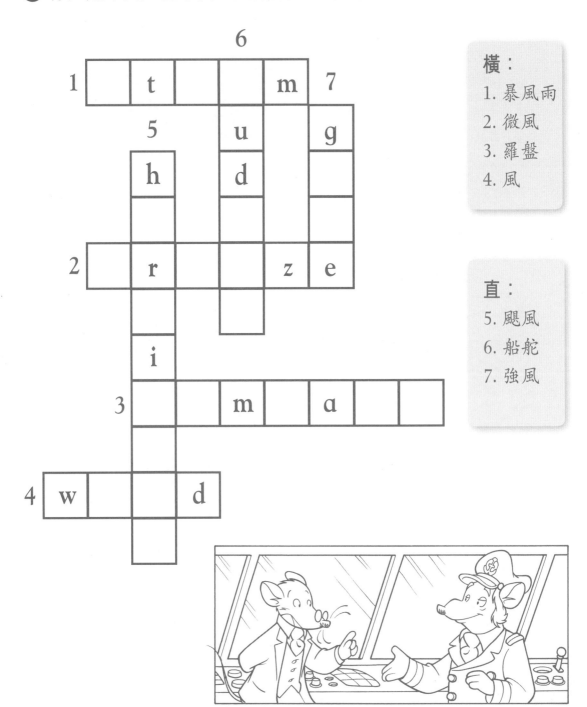

橫：
1. 暴風雨
2. 微風
3. 羅盤
4. 風

直：
5. 颶風
6. 船舵
7. 強風

THE SHIPWRECK 沉船

⭐ 謝利連摩他們在談論關於參觀沉船的事，想知道他們在說些什麼？從下面選出適當的字詞填在橫線上，完成他們的對話。

shipwreck　　divers　　sunk　　treasure　　ship

1.
Look! There's the ＿＿＿＿＿ over there!

2.
Was it a pirate ＿＿＿＿＿ carrying a treasure?

3.
It probably was. The ship ＿＿＿＿＿ .

4.
And the ＿＿＿＿＿ sunk, too?

5.
Yes, but ＿＿＿＿＿ found it a few years ago.

ANSWERS 答案

TEST 小測驗

1. (a) fishing boat   (b) ferry   (c) motorboat   (d) cruise ship   (e) sailing boat
2. (a) 這裏有超過100艘船。   (b) 這兒是妙鼠城海港！
   (c) 魚缸裏有數以百計的魚兒。   (d) 企鵝是出色的游泳員。
3. (a) two hundred and two   (b) two hundred and twenty   (c) two hundred and forty
   (d) two hundred and fifty   (e) one hundred and three   (f) one hundred and one
   (g) four hundred and five   (h) six hundred and seven   (i) one million
4. (a) 螺旋槳   (b) 舷窗   (c) 甲板   (d) 救生艇   (e) 船艙

EXERCISE BOOK 練習冊

P.1

1. ferry   2. fishing boat   3. tugboat   4. cruise ship   5. sailing boat   6. motorboat

P.2

1. boat, sea, because, storm   2. calm, fishing, go, fish

P.3

1. hundred   2. ten   3. twenty   4. thirty   5. forty   6. fifty   7. sixty   8. seventy
9. eighty   10. ninety   11. two   12. three   13. four   14. five   15. thousand
16. ten   17. hundred   18. million

P.4

1. aquarium, fish   2. hundreds   3. Penguins   4. turtles

P.5

1. funnel   2. deck   3. lifeboat
4. porthole   5. propeller

P.7

1. shipwreck   2. ship   3. sunk
4. treasure   5. divers

P.6

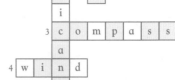